This book belongs to

....

For Mia and Rosie.
The most magical of folk. — **M.E.**

First published in the United States in 2024 by Welbeck Editions
An Imprint of Hachette Children's Books,
Part of Hodder & Stoughton Limited
Carmelite House, 50 Victoria Embankment
London EC4Y 0DZ

An Hachette UK Company
www.hachette.co.uk
www.hachettechildrens.co.uk

Text © 2024 Maz Evans
Illustration © 2024 Robert Ingpen

ISBN 978 1 80338 188 6

Printed in China

1 3 5 7 9 10 8 6 4 2

FSC
www.fsc.org
MIX
Paper | Supporting
responsible forestry
FSC® C104740

THE HIDDEN WORLD OF
MYTHICAL FOLK

Written by
MAZ EVANS

Illustrated by
ROBERT INGPEN

WELBECK
EDITIONS

As we grow, we find our lives become busy with the rattle and rush of the here and now. But the wisest of us know that sometimes it does us good to escape for a few precious moments, at those most magic times of day, into the woods of childhood that lie across the stream of time and over the hills of memory. We think of them as a half-remembered dream, and we long for those seemingly endless summer days, sweet-scented twilights and starlit nights. We can enter these places at will; we need only the power of our own imagination. And there are many pathways into that world from the road that leads from childhood to old age. These woods are endless and contain a hidden world we can visit, but we can only imagine what we can expect to find there. For here live those half-seen spirits that can delight, upset or curse you, from Scottish sprites and Irish leprechauns to fearsome Nordic trolls and Alpine barbegazi.

Let this book be your guide to recognizing friend from foe, so that you might walk those sylvan paths in safety and wonder. Let us begin with the fairy...

FAIRY

To define a fairy by their wings is akin to describing a falcon by its toenails or a dragon by its eyelashes – a curious disservice to a far more complex creature.

But it pleases our human eyes to see them thus, and so this is how a fairy will usually manifest, with gossamer wings and magic wands and glittering dust. Though, they laugh at the fools who delight in such fripperies.

For a fairy's real power is a potent thing and not to be trifled with. Naturally mischievous creatures, fairies are capable of bestowing great pleasure or worse pain. For those they favor, they will rearrange the stars to serve your hopes and dreams on a moonbeam. For those they dislike... well, you would be wise not to find out.

GOBLIN

It's not always easy to spot a goblin, as they assume a human form when moving among us. But if you stray away from the hustle and bustle of human life, you may chance upon one. But please take care if you do. While some magical folk possess both light and dark powers, goblins are only capable of trouble.

There's no need to take their malice personally, because they simply delight in causing a little chaos whenever the opportunity arises. There's only so much damage they can do – their abilities are limited to luck-spoiling and the weaving of nightmares.

But discretion is the better part of valor, so do take care. Especially if you need a good night's sleep before looking for a four-leaf clover.

ELF

If imitation is the highest form of flattery, humans should find elves endlessly complimentary. However, the similarities are merely physical. These impressive creatures seem to have avoided many of the pitfalls that hold humans back.

Elves attach little importance to beauty – although that is easy when you carry so much of it – or to material possessions, preferring instead to celebrate the wealth of the natural world. They commit their immortal lives to the pursuit of wisdom and have used their vast knowledge of the past to confidently and accurately predict the future.

None of us is perfect, however, and elves can be predisposed to a little superiority regarding the rest of creation. We might say, 'You're snobby.' And they'd likely reply, 'You're silly.'

RAINBOW SERPENT

The Australian landscape is as old as the spirits that created its rocks, hills, streams and waterfalls. And it is still awakening from where it all began.

In Aboriginal Australian mythology, the Rainbow Serpent is responsible for the creation of rivers and continues to keep watch over its waters. But just as a rainbow requires both sunshine and rain, this serpent has two opposing sides. When at peace, it refreshes the land with flowing water and gentle drizzle. When agitated, violent thunder and vicious storms are unleashed from its multicolored coils.

There is no malice in these disturbances, they merely serve as a reminder of the power this spirit possesses. You might observe the serpent moving from one body of water to another in its rainbow form, a journey that never ceases to bring wonder and delight to all who bear witness.

GNOME

Conventional wisdom suggests that we should all work hard and play hard. To its credit, the global gnome population has enthusiastically adopted half of this mantra.

A diminutive version of whichever humans they live near, gnomes are incredibly hard-working creatures. They busy themselves with ensuring the natural world is just so. Their great hope is that once they finish their fixing, tidying, and building, they will retire into a carefree existence... but as with any chore, no sooner are they finished, that it's time to start them all over again.

However, everyone needs some downtime. When gnomes decide to take a break, they let off steam with days of wild singing and dancing, which might account for their incredibly long life spans. But in their quieter moments, nothing quite delights a gnome like decorating their garden with novelty statues of humans.

BOGGART

Domestic irritants are a daily part of life, but next time your keys aren't where you left them, or the cookies mysteriously vanish from the jar, bear in mind that you might be at the mercy of a boggart.

Since nobody really knows what they look like, they are not an easy pest to remove. They tend to lurk in dark places both inside and out; anywhere they can wreak their havoc. Once they've grown attached to a family, they will move around with them.

Some small precautionary measures can be taken – a horseshoe hung on the door can be a deterrent, as can salt heaped outside a bedroom door. But whatever you do, do not give your boggart a name. Once it has one, it becomes entirely unreasonable, completely uncontrollable and will refuse to leave your house.

BROWNIE

Now, if there's an infestation of magical folk you want in your home, it is the brownies. Not only do these Scottish sprites bring luck wherever they go, but they'll clean your home while they're at it.

Tread softly, though, for they are easily offended. Do not insult them or take them for granted — and whatever you do, don't offer them clothing to replace their rags. Such a slight will send them away forever ... or worse, turn them into a boggart in a fit of rage.

Brownies are strictly nocturnal, performing their chores under cover of night. Almost exclusively male, they won't trouble you for a place to stay, preferring instead the solace of a nearby cave or stream. They require little in return for their services; all they desire is a bowl of milk or a little bread left by the hearth. And, unlike most family members, they'll even clean up their own dishes afterward.

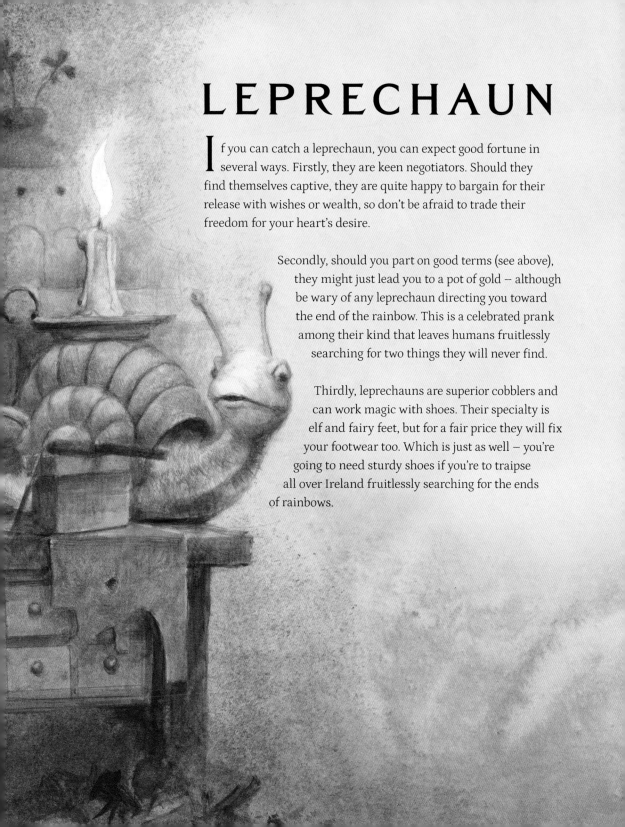

LEPRECHAUN

If you can catch a leprechaun, you can expect good fortune in several ways. Firstly, they are keen negotiators. Should they find themselves captive, they are quite happy to bargain for their release with wishes or wealth, so don't be afraid to trade their freedom for your heart's desire.

Secondly, should you part on good terms (see above), they might just lead you to a pot of gold – although be wary of any leprechaun directing you toward the end of the rainbow. This is a celebrated prank among their kind that leaves humans fruitlessly searching for two things they will never find.

Thirdly, leprechauns are superior cobblers and can work magic with shoes. Their specialty is elf and fairy feet, but for a fair price they will fix your footwear too. Which is just as well – you're going to need sturdy shoes if you're to traipse all over Ireland fruitlessly searching for the ends of rainbows.

TROLL

Harkening from the rocky outcrops of the Scandinavian wilderness, trolls are one of the magical world's more misunderstood creatures. This is largely thanks to their unfair representation in certain fairy stories. There are no records of any trolls living under bridges, nor terrorizing billy goats – they are, in fact, rather solitary creatures and are strictly vegetarian.

They enjoy the great outdoors, freely roaming the forests and fjords of their northern homelands. There have been few sightings from which one can gain a meaningful description. Those who claim to have spotted a troll report large, indistinct forms with a strangely human appearance.

Some say trolls enjoy scaring humans during the long summer nights, but this is little more than an unsubstantiated rumor. And chiefly from the kind of people who believe in talking billy goats.

LESHY

Those who claim Slavic ancestry will be familiar with the leshy. Indeed, they may have encountered one in the forests, for every woodland has its own leshy. Like many mythical folk, they are elusive, their features often undefined in stories. This is perhaps because of their ability to shape-shift at will, their bodies in tune with the changing rhythms of the forests in which they dwell.

A leshy's benevolence will depend very much on you. If you are respectful of their sylvan surroundings, they will leave you in peace to go on your way.

Leshy have no tolerance for adults who do not take good care of their own children. Should a leshy become aware of any child in distress, they will whisk them away to their enchanted realm to live the happy life they deserve.

ABATWA

What the diminutive abatwa lack in height – the tallest among them is only half the height of a blade of grass – they certainly make up for in ability. Possessed of wisdom, skill and certain gifts of foresight, they are generally friends to us humans, dispensing wise counsel from the anthills that they frequent.

They are nomadic and practical creatures, moving from one place to the next on the back of a single steed. Ants are not only a highly efficient form of travel, but they become a very tasty one too, should the abatwa's hunting endeavors be fruitless.

Abatwas are shy – only very young, very magic or very pregnant people can commune with them and, should you wish to know the gender of your baby, an abatwa can reveal that secret. But be mindful that, like us all, they don't care to be offended. If you upset an abatwa in any way, they might use their age-old wisdom to reason with you. Or they might just fire a deadly poison arrow into your foot and bring the conversation to a swift conclusion.

BARBEGAZI

While many of us yearn for the warm summer months, barbegazi prefer to sleep through them, saving themselves for the icy winter chill in their French and Swiss mountain homes. Often mistaken for dwarves or gnomes, these taciturn creatures roam the slopes, with their large and flat feet helping them travel across the snow or tunnel beneath it.

Like many magical folk, barbegazi – whose name derives from the French *barbes glacées* or 'frozen beards' – take care of those who take care of their home. Treat their mountain environment with respect and they might just save your life – their particular dialect of whistles has been known to warn climbers of impending avalanches or guide help towards them.

But get on the wrong side of a barbegazi or treat their mountains carelessly ... when you need help, frankly, you can whistle for it.

SHREW

Folklore, like all histories, is rarely kind to unconventional women. And so it is for Dulle Griet of Ghent, who was perhaps the first 'shrew', if such a term must be bestowed.

Depicted in a famous painting by the Flemish artist Pieter Bruegel the Elder, Dulle Griet took it upon herself to lay siege to hell itself, in order to rid the world of the evils it produces. Armed with a breastplate and wielding a frying pan, this no-nonsense heroine sought out the devil with an army of like-minded women. According to a local proverb, 'Against six women, the devil himself has no weapon'.

Alas, this proved untrue. Dulle Griet's campaign was unsuccessful on all fronts – both hell and her unjust reputation endured. Many have misunderstood her actions through the ages. But to others among us, the urge to go on a warring rampage armed only with a kitchen utensil is painfully, and heroically, relatable.

DWARF

Not to be confused with gnomes — to do so is to cause great and lasting offense — dwarfs can be found all around the globe, but are most populous in Germanic nations. They are small in stature but big in presence. Simply get on their bad side (by calling them 'gnomes', for instance) to experience the mighty wrath of their mightier magic.

But, by and large, the dwarf population is happy to keep to itself, leaving humans to their follies while they get on with their greater preoccupation — metalwork. There isn't a metallurgic substance that a dwarf can't mine and then craft into something powerful. Weapons, rings, armor... their skill is unmatched in the magical world.

They have no comprehension of war, seeing it as nonsense, and thus have no need for the weaponry they craft. But they understand money perfectly well and will happily sell their wares to the highest bidder, believing wealth to be the greatest victory of all.

KNOCKER

Anyone who has worked in the mining industry will know how challenging the profession can be. They will also be well aware of the benefits of having a friendly knocker on your side.

These subterranean souls frequent mines around the world, their small form allowing them to move easily through the narrow tunnels. Their name derives from their ability to alert miners to new seams by faintly tapping on the walls. Ignore these signals at your peril, however – the knockers can also forewarn of impending collapse.

They ask little by way of return. Cornish knockers will gladly take the last piece of your pasty crust as payment, but any foodstuffs are gratefully received. And it's as well to settle your account. For if you choose not to pay the knockers with your lunch, the chances are they'll just steal it from you anyway.

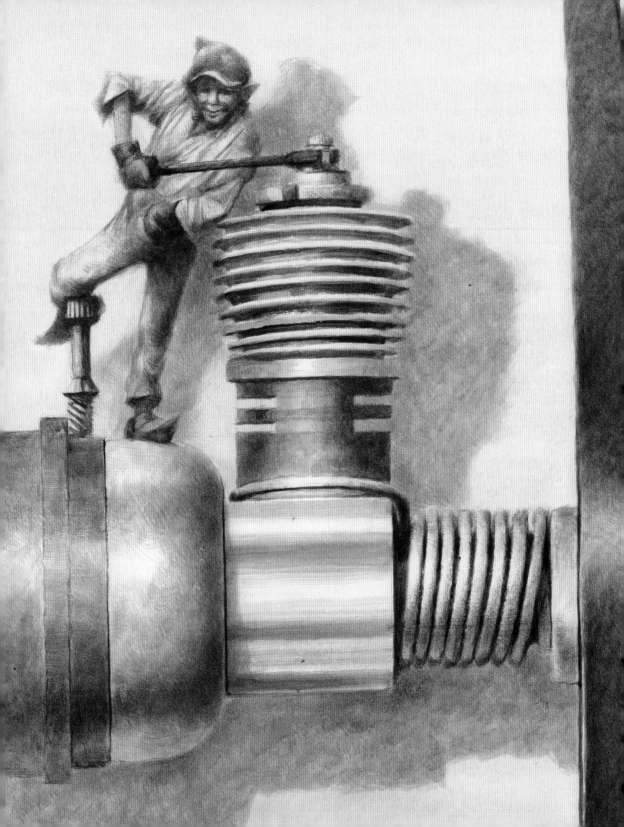

GREMLIN

Another species whose reputation has fallen victim to the worst of their kind, gremlins are in fact largely helpful creatures whose main purpose is to fix tools and machinery.

Gremlins are skilled mechanics who can, quite literally, get inside any machine. They are also a handy friend to have in a crisis, able as they are to quickly fix most human devices.

But, as is often the way, the actions of a minority have sullied the good works of the majority. Not all gremlins are so benevolent or helpful – a rebel few take great joy in burning the toast, stealing a single sock or letting the air out of tires. Sadly, it is these gremlins who get the headlines, especially when they have had their wicked way with train engineering works or rush-hour traffic.

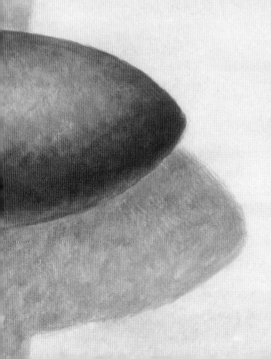

KOBOLD

Few magical folk have migrated as successfully as the kobold and their presence can be felt in many places – in mines, aboard ships and within many households, where they quietly perform housework in return for their quiet board and lodging.

Kobold can be good friends or troublesome adversaries. They can manifest as humans, animals, objects or even fire – and none of those are to be toyed with lightly.

The kobold's original and preferred home is an orchard, where they will happily take charge of the ripening and blossoming of fruit to ensure a perfect bite. It is rumored that, beneath the trees they tend so carefully, lies buried treasure that they are also determined to nurture. And so when a kobold offers you a Golden Delicious, you can be sure they know exactly what they are doing.

REDCAP

It is sometimes unclear what motivates the redcap – but reason is of little consequence should you happen to meet one along the Anglo-Scottish border.

There's nothing redcaps enjoy more than the wanton destruction of anyone who crosses their path. Should you take refuge in an abandoned castle or watchtower in this region, a redcap will gladly pelt you with rocks until you meet a miserable end. And – not that you're likely to care much for their fashion sense at this point – they will dye their caps red with your blood.

There are measures that can be taken to ward off a redcap. They cannot be overcome with human strength, but speak words from a sacred text to them and they will burst into flames rather than hear them (leaving only a large tooth as evidence of their presence). An example, if ever it were needed, of the pen being mightier than the sword.

BASAJAUN

While many magical folk can be tricky to spot given their small stature, you'd struggle to miss a basajaun. The smallest among them are taller than the tallest human.

Roaming the hills and forests of the Basque regions, the basajaun are gentle giants, and, highly skilled in invention, they devote many of their creations to agricultural progression. They are particular friends to shepherds and will ring distinctive bells or simply whistle loudly when danger approaches the flock in the form of storms or predators.

Unassuming as the basajaun are, they ask little in return for this service. A piece of bread will suffice for their labors – and to ensure they don't trouble you unduly, they'll even collect their reward when you are asleep.

ANKOU

Roaming the roads at night is a fool's errand at the best of times, but, should you find yourself in Brittany, take particular care – for this is where the spectral ankou dwell.

These tall, gaunt servants of death wander the highways and byways of their home, driving a cart drawn by pale honey-coloured horses and accompanied by two figures who drift behind. Not a word is spoken, nor a sound uttered. Like the master they serve, you won't ever hear them coming.

They make for a ghoulish and discomforting display – but that's not the only reason you wouldn't want to encounter them on your travels. For should you hear the clatter of hooves and cartwheels, the purpose of their journey will become painfully clear. They have come to take your soul to the afterlife. And the ankou only offer one-way rides.

KAPPA

The water can be a dangerous place, but never more so than when a kappa lurks on a Japanese riverbed, awaiting its prey from the unsuspecting swimmers above.

Now considered extremely rare, kappa are as curious as they are deadly. A hybrid creature with the legs of a frog, the head of a monkey and the shell of a turtle, this sea-monster's head is hollow and filled with water. Should that water be emptied, the kappa becomes vulnerable, meaning that it generally sticks to the relative safety of the murky underwaters.

But not always. Nothing delights the kappa more than trapping and drowning swimmers who stray too far from the shores, for no better reason than its own sport. Thankfully, the kappa has not been seen for many years, and some consider it extinct. But take care. Like so much evil, just because you can't see it, it doesn't mean it is not there.

GENIE

It is unclear who first thought to imprison a genie in a lamp, or why they did so. But should you come across one, this is unlikely to be your first question. You will probably prefer, as most do, to get straight down to having your greatest wishes granted.

Genies are believed to have been created long ago from magical smokeless fire. They are naturally impish, so it is possible that it is their own transgressions that led to their capture. It is equally likely that pure human greed trapped these beings in lamps at the very moment their potential was realized.

But with genies, as with all things, be careful what you wish for. Contrary to popular perception, genies aren't actually obliged to grant you whatever you seek. And don't even try wishing for more wishes. They'll most likely hide back in their lamp until someone more interesting comes along.

DRYADS

As if nature wasn't stunning enough in its own right, certain woodlands have improved upon perfection with a population of dryads – the beautiful nymphs of the trees.

Bonded by enchantment to the tree in which they reside, dryads were originally only found in oak trees. They have since broadened their horizons, inhabiting trees that befit their personalities, be they willowy, thorny or even something of a puzzle. But the relationship is symbiotic – should the tree or its dryad be harmed or perish, the other is endangered too.

Dryads are benevolent folk but incredibly shy, usually transforming into a sapling at the sight of a human. But make sure you never harm their trees, for even the greatest beauty can turn ugly when their home is under threat.

EL NIÑO

While the natural world is largely very tolerant of its human guests, every now and again it likes to remind them who owns the house. El Niño keeps a literal weather eye on our behaviors in its oceans.

This Peruvian sea-spirit is at heart very mild-mannered, bringing rain and tropical waters to where they are most needed. Fishermen have historically been grateful for El Niño's bounty, the fluctuations in oceanic temperature ensuring that they fill their nets all year round.

But like us all, El Niño has its limits. When people push their luck, El Niño pushes back, summoning up storms to put us firmly back in our place and remind us that when humans take on nature, there will only ever be one winner.

BLACK ANNIS

It is the sad case for many mythological folk that their true intentions have been ignored, instead replaced by human rumor and untruths. But when it comes to Black Annis, alas, there is little room for interpretation.

Roaming the open spaces of northern England and the Scottish Highlands, her name is the first trick she likes to play. For Black Annis is in fact entirely blue, perhaps from the freezing cold blood that runs through her veins as she perpetrates her terrible crimes.

Her single eye seeks out her victims, as Black Annis loves nothing more than the taste of human flesh, especially that of children. Young people from her hunting grounds are warned to be good, lest she feasts on them. But this simply isn't true. Black Annis just isn't that discerning – she'll happily devour you whole, no matter how you behave.

PIXIE

Forget all that you've been told about these 'enchanting' magical folk – pixies are menaces, as any traveler who has encountered one will happily concur.

Though tiny, these pests contain a vast amount of mischief. They spend their days seeking out lone wanderers to lead astray, and will then laugh as the target roams hopelessly around the countryside.

These days, pixies have moved with the times and vex weary travelers with more modern methods – traffic jams, poor signage and inaccurate satnavs are among their favorite tricks. But the age-old method to repel them remains the same: simply wear your coat inside out and they will have no choice but to leave you in peace. As will most other folk you encounter.

PUCK

While most magical folk are clear in their good or bad intentions, with a puck, you can never be entirely sure where you stand.

Mainly found in rural, southern England, pucks resemble – but thankfully are not entirely related to – pixies. They rub along happily with most other fae and fairy folk and can be a great help to humans, quietly carrying on with housework or simply serenading them with lilting music as they sleep.

However, there is another, less sociable side to a puck, who is capable of great mischief should the mood take them. It's unclear what prompts this naughtiness. It seems to have nothing to do with human behavior – this is not a punishment, more a sport. But if a leaky faucet or missing shoe is giving you a bad day, it is safe to assume that a nearby puck is having a good one.

WIZARD

One of the magical realm's most respected – and feared – inhabitants, wizards are only slightly younger than magic itself. And should be treated equally as cautiously.

Often associated with witches, wizards are in fact entirely their own beings – and often not nearly as benign as their misunderstood female colleagues. Like witches, they do call upon the natural world to practice their spells, but the magic they summon is generally used for harm rather than healing, particularly favoring turning their enemies into toads.

Not all wizards are so like-minded, however. Some have chosen to use their gifts for good and have been rewarded for their wisdom with gainful employment in the courts of queens and kings. But it's as well to stay on the right side of their wands. Unless, of course, you enjoy the taste of flies for breakfast.

GLOSSARY

AFTERLIFE - life after death

AGRICULTURAL - relating to farming

BENEVOLENCE - kindness

BENIGN - describes someone who is gentle and mild

BREASTPLATE - a piece of armor covering the chest

BRITTANY - a region in northwest France

COBBLER - a shoe-repairer

COMPREHENSION - the ability to understand something

DERIVE - to obtain something from

DIALECT - a variation of a language, spoken by a particular group of people

DIMINUTIVE - unusually small

DISCERNING - able to recognise and understand something

DISCRETION - the right to decide something

DISTINCTIVE - possessing a unique or different characteristic

FAE - a magical and fairylike creature

FORESIGHT - the ability to predict what will happen in the future

FRIPPERIES - showy or unnecessarily ornamental things

GERMANIC - relating to the German-speaking peoples

GHOULISH - resembling a ghoul

GOSSAMER - a fine, delicate substance (like cobwebs)

HEROINE - a woman admired for her courage

HOLLOW - having an empty space inside

HUE - a color or shade

HYBRID - a combination

IMPENDING - about to happen

IMPISH - inclined to do slightly naughty things

INTENTION - an idea of what you are going to do

IRRITANT - something that is constantly annoying or distracting

MALICE - wrongful intention

MANIPULATION - when someone tries to influence you to get what they want

MENACE - something that threatens to cause evil

MIGRATED - moved from one area to another

NOCTURNAL - active at night

NOMAD - someone who travels from place to place

NURTURE - to care for and protect

NYMPHS - female nature spirits from Greek mythology

PERIL - serious and immediate danger

PERISH - to die

PROFESSION - a paid job

PROVERB - a short, well-known saying that teaches you something about life

RAMPAGE - to move through a place in a violent manner

RURAL - the countryside, or an open area of land with few homes or buildings

SACRED - dedicated to a religious purpose, and so deserving respect

SAPLING - a young tree

SERENADE - to sing or play a song for someone

SOLITARY - existing alone

SUBTERRANEAN - below the Earth's surface

SUFFICE - to be enough

SYLVAN - associated with woodland

SYMBIOTIC - a close relationship between two different living things

UNDULY - more than is necessary

UNSUBSTANTIATED - not supported by evidence

VEGETARIAN - a person who does not eat meat or fish

VULNERABLE - exposed to the possibility of being harmed

THE HIDDEN WORLD OF
MAGICAL
CREATURES

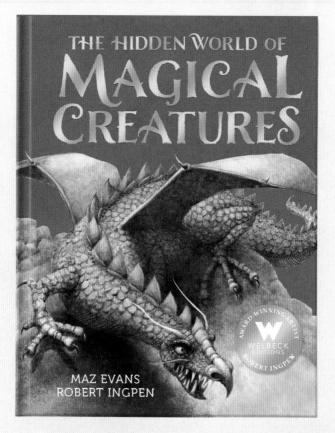

Maz Evans & Robert Ingpen

In this stunning guide, discover the world's most beloved magical creatures.
From the heart of a forest, in the deepest sea, on the highest mountains of
the world, and in the darkest caves, mystical beasts and helpful spirits have
inspired countless legends passed down from generation to generation.